D0412928

THIS BLOOMSBURY BOOK

BELONGS TO

....

For Harry Sellen, with love — SR
To my dear friend Nick — JN

First published in Great Britain in 2000 by Bloomsbury Publishing Plc
38 Soho Square, London W1V 5DF

Text copyright © Shen Roddie 2000
Illustrations copyright © Jill Newton 2000
The moral right of the author and illustrator has been asserted.

All rights reserved.
No part of this publication may be reproduced
or transmitted by any means, electronic, mechanical, photocopying
or otherwise without the prior permission of the publisher.

A CIP catalogue record for this book is available from the British Library.
ISBN 0 7475 4484 0

Designed by Dawn Apperley

Printed and bound in Hong Kong / China by South China Printing Co.

1 3 5 7 9 10 8 6 4 2

Please Don't Chat to the Bus Driver

Shen Roddie and Jill Newton

BLOOMSBURY
CHILDREN'S
BOOKS

Here comes the bus! Up you go, Pig.

But please don't chat to the Bus Driver.
"I won't," said Pig.

But she did!

And the bus missed a stop!

Here comes the bus that missed a stop.
Up you go, Croc.

But please don't chat to the Bus Driver!
"I won't," said Croc.

But he did!
And the bus hit a post-box!

Here comes the battered bus that missed a stop. Up you go, Rabbit! But please don't chat to the Bus Driver!
"I won't," said Rabbit.

But he did!
And the Bus Driver fell fast asleep!

Here comes the late, battered bus that missed a stop. Up you go, Fox.

But please don't chat to the Bus Driver!
"I won't," said Fox.

But he did!

And the Bus Driver fell on his horn, laughing! Honk, Honk blared the horn!

Here comes the noisy, late, battered bus that missed a stop. Up you go, Hen.

But please don't chat to the Bus Driver!
"I won't," said Hen.

But she did!
And the dizzy Bus Driver spun
round and round the roundabout!

Here comes the spinning, noisy, late,
battered bus that missed a stop.
Up you go, Cow.

But please don't chat to the Bus Driver!
"I won't," said Cow.

But she did!
And the bus went the wrong way!

Here comes the lost, spinning, noisy, late, battered bus that missed a stop.
Up you go, Frog!

But please don't chat to the Bus Driver!
"I won't," said Frog.

But he did! And the bus shot over
a hump and lost a wheel!

The limping, lost, spinning, noisy, late, battered bus that missed a stop, stopped!

"All out!" shouted the Bus Driver.
Everybody scrambled out.

Here comes the next bus. Up you go,
everyone! And remember —

don't chat to the Bus Driver!

"We won't," said Pig, Croc, Rabbit,
Fox, Hen, Cow and Frog.

But they did!

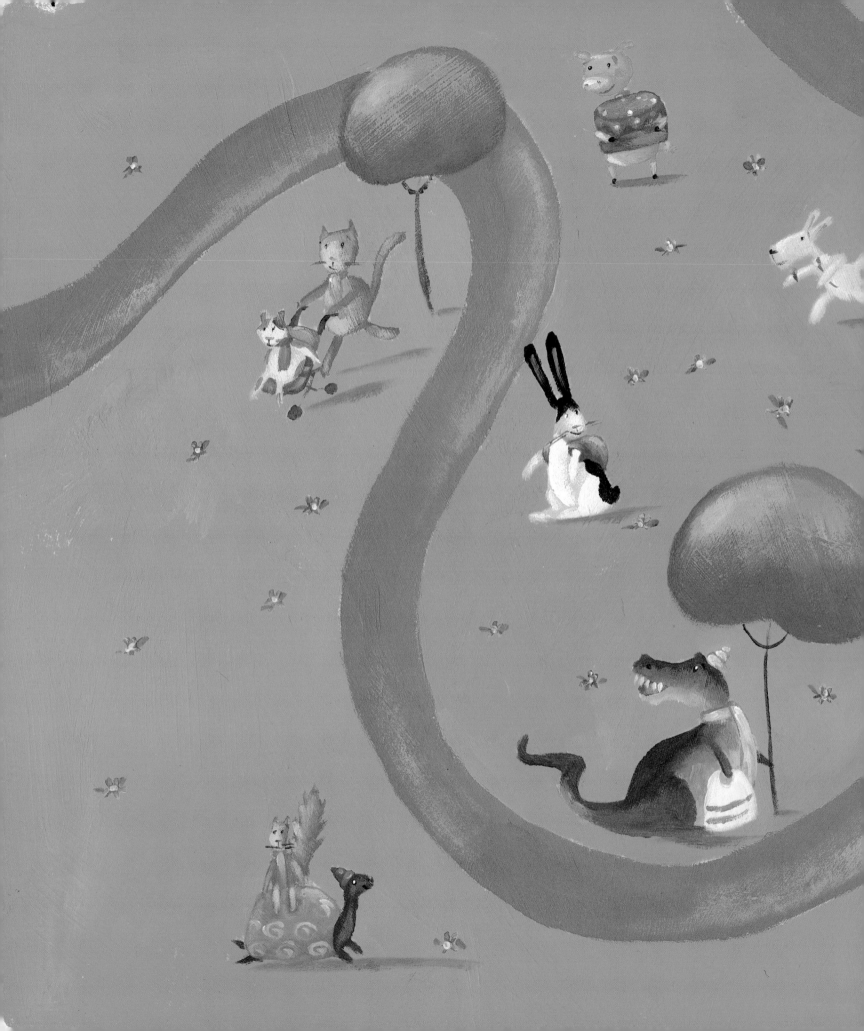